Contents

POINTS NORTH

Short Stories by Scottish Writers
Edited by Lindsey Fraser

mammoth

First published in Great Britain in 2000 by Mammoth,
an imprint of Egmont Children's Books Limited,
a division of Egmont Holding Limited,
239 Kensington High Street, London W8 6SA

ISBN 0 7497 4034 5

10 9 8 7 6 5 4 3 2 1

A CIP catalogue record for this book is available from the British Library

Printed in Great Britain by Cox & Wyman Ltd, Reading, Berkshire

CONTENTS

No Ordinary Zombie   1
Julie Bertagna

Those Other Mountains   16
Dilys Rose

Ghost Track   31
Chris Dolan

Notes in the Margin   48
Theresa Breslin

Time Table   56
Candia McWilliam

The Five Sisters of Kintail   66
Jackie Kay

Granny's Books   81
Gordon Legge

The Story of Major Cartwright, by Murdo   96
Iain Crichton Smith

Clearing my Head   102
Lindsey Fraser

Biographical notes   116

No Ordinary
Zombie

Julie Bertagna

She was   cave.
        no ordinary   no ordinary
            spider.   And this was
                It was   web.
                no ordinary

                            Down
                            off
                            the web
                            down
                            deep
                            into
                            the dark
                            of the
                            cave
                            the
                            spider
                            d
                            r
                            o
                            p
                            p
                            e
                            d.

Deserting a banquet of insects, blind to the beauty of the vast web, the spider ran straight towards a body that lay in the darkest pocket of the cave. Up the motionless arm, up on to its face she ran, as if dragged by the silken thread of her own spinnerets. When she reached the mouth the spider dropped into its black, unbreathing hole.

The web shuddered. The silence broke. A cry poured into the dark – a cry to crack open centuries. The body twitched, convulsed and rolled violently about the belly of the cave. Then sat bolt upright, leaned forwards and retched. Retched again, violently punching itself in the gut with a thin fist until at last in a dry, dusty vomit it emptied itself of the spider.

The body staggered to its feet, stamping dementedly, mashing all sorts of blameless insects. (But not the spider. She had scuttled back up on the body, run up a hairy leg and was now secreting herself in the sporran of its kilt.)

The body in the kilt leaned against the cave wall. He had not felt the spider. But now he felt something else. Its vast presence was all around him: something hoary, ancient and impending. It was the web, the ancient web that the spider, her mother, her grandmothers and countless generations of her spider clan had laboured on, century upon century. Now it covered the entire innards of Robert the Bruce's legendary cave. Now, at last, it was complete. And now the zombie was roused.

Fossil-thoughts flew about the zombie's head, whirling like the ancient dust he had disturbed in the cave. How long had he been here? He had no idea. Words stuck in his throat like dead insects. His voice crackled with dust, a death rattle in reverse.

The zombie staggered into the great web that hung like a shroud across the cave mouth. In a split second he smashed through the work of a thousand generations. And with the umpteenth great-granddaughter of Robert the Bruce's legendary spider a stowaway in the sporran of his kilt, the zombie reeled out of the cave and made straight for the great arm of tarmac that reached towards the city like a yearning.

Words are sometimes not enough. How can thin, ordinary words tell you of the dark bandit force – the sheer tattered menace – of a zombie charging on to an empty motorway in the murky half-light of dawn? There are moments when the world shudders. Lurching moments in time when the future balances on a silken thread and the nerve channels that map the globe like a vast web tremble. It was that kind of a moment.

The zombie stepped on to the motorway, right into the path of the only vehicle on the road that morning. A lorryload of nuclear warheads bulleting north screamed into a skid and came within a hair's breadth of smashing into a wall of solid rock. The shocked, coffee-sharpened driver will never forget that moment of near carnage at daybreak one Thursday, just beyond Edinburgh, when a zombie covered in spider web took the full force of a stack of Trident missiles, and walked away.

He had lost the spider. Somewhere in Princes Street. She'd been sitting peacefully enough up his sleeve in the bookshop where he'd been catching up on the seven hundred years of history he'd slept through. Then in the burger bar she'd taken a wander and he'd had to fish her out of one of the leftover Cokes he'd scavenged. Somewhere between there and here she'd gone missing. She was a restless one, that spider.

The zombie had discovered his stowaway soon after his collision with the Trident missiles. Sitting by the roadside, slightly dazed and wondering which direction he should take, he saw the spider scuttle out of his kilt sporran. In seconds she had spun a tiny, perfect web in the crease of his elbow. Opening the sporran, he had found it stuffed full of the finest, most stubborn of cobwebs. The zombie knew at once that his stowaway was one of that tenacious, legendary clan. No ordinary spider ever spun such inspired gossamer so ferociously, so unstoppably, with such fated certainty. He'd set her down upon the road then, ready to follow wherever her instinct tugged. In this way, the spider had led him to the city.

The road. He'd crossed the road twice, hadn't he, to get away from the young ones who'd been bothering him all afternoon. The zombie headed back along Princes Street, searching for the lost spider. People stared at the strangeness of him, at the trapped violence in his walk. It was as if he were trying to flee a great weight that kept him grounded. He stepped out into the fierce stream of traffic and began examining the tarmac. Horns and yells couldn't budge him, not even the hard whack of a passing bus – he just resettled his head back upon his neck and went on searching. It was only when he heard the police siren that he gave up and ran off into Princes Street Gardens. And came face to face with his tormentors again – the three young ones who had been tailing him, baiting him, laughing at him, nothing better to do with their time.

'Lost something?' asked the boy with a face as sharp as flint.

'My spider,' said the zombie.

They fell about laughing. Then, unexpectedly, the girl seemed to take pity on him.

'I like spiders. I'll help you look for him.'

'Her,' said the zombie, and they all fell about laughing, again.

They were persistent. They were loud and cruel. They were only having fun. Kilt-flicking and shin-kicking progressed into hard shoves and punches. The zombie took it all until he had them in a lone spot on a stretch of grass that lay in the shadow of the castle. Then he turned and hit them with a full-on zombie stare. He watched them reel back from the abyss in his eyes and smelled the animal fear in them. Then he grinned a black, desperate grin. It was a long time since he'd had any fun.

'He's mental,' panicked the flint-faced boy.

'Zoid,' said the other, a squat one with cheeks of fire.

'Acid head,' said the girl.

The tormentors backed off, attempting to keep their cool. But the zombie was just warming up. He'd forgotten how it was to be a zombie in the world, one of the living dead. He had been asleep far too long. He was about to rip the skin off his face, pop out an eye, dislocate his hip or maybe his neck to see how they liked that when the girl did something far more shocking. She stepped forward and touched him. Just a fleeting touch on his shoulder. Then she jumped back.

'What *is* that?' she said.

The zombie looked at the sheen of cobweb upon his shoulder. The girl's fingers had rested there for less than a second but he had seen her nails, black and shiny like beetles. It was the first time anyone, other than the spider, had touched him in over seven centuries.

'Spider web,' he said. (Plus a strip or two of the dead skin that was forever peeling off, but he would ignore that for the moment.)

'You're covered in it,' said the girl.

'Yes,' said the zombie. He couldn't take his eyes off the girl. The eyes that stared back at him were ringed with blackness and were as blue as the cold sky above the castle, as blue as the Saltire flag that fluttered there. She looked deathly, her face covered in white powder, lips black and shiny like the beetle nails. Her hair was beetle black too, as black as midnight in the ancient cave. Once, he had dreamed of such a girl. But he had come to believe there were none. He had never met another of his kind.

The zombie imagined the girl covered in cobweb and dust, lying beside him in the cave. 'You are beautiful,' he said.

The boys yelled with laughter. The girl froze. She stepped forward again and this time she shoved the zombie with a force that scattered the dead skin and tore the spider web from his shoulder. The action made the zombie wonder if she was really his kind after all. There was so much life in her.

'Beat it, acid head.' The girl wiped her hands clean of spider web and stomped off.

He thought about her all night. He wandered the castle grounds, thinking of her – the girl who looked like one of his kind, deathly, with beetle lips and midnight hair and black-rimmed eyes the colour of the Saltire. Was she the destiny the spider had led him to, the one who might release him from the prison of living death? A surge ran through him, a dizzying free-fall sensation, as if the stagnant blood in his veins had begun to race with life. The zombie sank his teeth into his arm, piercing the skin, just to see. But no blood ran. Of course it didn't. It never would.

He searched the city ferociously for her. His search for the spider was all but forgotten. Then at last, up on the castle walls, he found her.

'It's spiderman,' a voice called.

'Oy, Kirsten, loverboy's back,' said another.

The flint-faced boy and the squat one with the cheeks on fire stood between him and the girl. Why did they have to be here too? The zombie longed to be alone with the girl, here, up on the castle on this dull, dank evening. *Kirsten*. He breathed the word into the damp air, made a mist cloud of her name. She was watching him. There was wariness, disgust perhaps, on her face. And a shudder of interest.

'Found your spider?' she asked slyly. Nastily even. It only made him love her more.

'I must find her,' said the zombie. 'She is the spider of all spiders. A spider among millions. The key to my destiny.'

'What a zoid,' said the fire-cheeked one. 'Out of his face.'

'She led me to you,' the zombie told the girl.

But the other two had started on him again, yanking up his kilt, baiting him. Then the boy with the fire-cheeks took a matchbox from his pocket.

'The spider of all spiders, a spider among millions, must be worth at least a tenner.' The boy slid the matchbox cover open and there she was. The zombie could have picked her out from all the spiders in the world.

The boy closed the lid, chucked the matchbox on the ground and placed his foot over it. 'A tenner and she's yours. Or I'll mash her.'

The zombie had another blood-rush sensation, the second since he'd woken from his sleep of centuries. Not love this time but anger surged inside, anger that had slept for seven hundred years. He grabbed the boy with a force that lifted him off the ground. He would smash the tormenting brute down the steep cliffside, on to the train track below . . . he could hear a train on its way from Waverley Station.

The girl's scream pierced him as keenly as her eyes. Pierced him in the place his heart would beat were he truly alive, not trapped in this either-or existence. He put the boy down. The fire cheeks had paled to ash. A strip of zombie skin lay curled upon the arm of the boy's leather jacket. The boy saw it and screamed. He flung the skin away, shuddering. The girl put the matchbox in the zombie's hand, shuddering too, careful not to make contact with his peeling skin. But she looked him in the eyes.

'What are you?' she whispered as she backed away and he knew she had seen the true depth of his abyss, the never-ending nothingness that was his life. A deathly life. His living death.

The zombie flung the spider from him. He couldn't stand it any more. The abyss inside him was not his own. It belonged to the whole city, the whole of the land, to its living and its dead. The zombie was the place where all the dead dreams and lost chances had come to live. He was not made of flesh and blood – but of lost, dead things.

The train passed the castle, the sound of it bulleting off the volcanic cliff and the ancient stone. The sound galvanised the zombie and he clambered up on to the castle wall.

The moment lurched beneath his feet. He balanced upon it, feeling its endless possibilities map like a trembling web all around and out beyond him, far out into the world, out into the past, the present and the future. He must choose, *now*. Life or death. Or hang for ever in this sticky trap of either-or. The zombie reeled between the girl and the abyss below him. Then he chose.

He jumped.

The girl's touch was what he longed for as he smashed into the solid rock wall of cliff.

Up at the castle they saw the ten thousand-volt explosion as the zombie crashed off the cliff and hit the electric power line above the train track. They heard the terrible cry as his life cracked open and the lost, dead things poured out of the abyss. Their keening wails rose up and swirled round the castle. The echo would hang there like a vast cobweb, for all time.

The girl found the zombie crawling off the railway line below the castle. He collapsed at her feet, lifelessly. The blasted beauty of him shocked her. When she kneeled beside him she saw the hot blue pulse on his neck. She touched it and his eyes opened. He sat up and a cascade of dead skin flew from him. He was new, raw, weightless. He was amazed. Desires and fears and dreams sparked and crackled in the place where the abyss had been.

'What are you?' gasped the girl, though what she saw told her he was one of her kind.

'I'm alive,' said the ordinary man who was once a zombie.

Centuries smashed into dust. The future derailed. But in the split moment that was here, now, two people reeled towards the rage of life each met in the other's eyes.

While up in a corner of the castle the spider spun a new web.

Those Other Mountains

'I hate your guts!'

'I hate yours!'

'Fatface!'

'Frizzhead!'

Rene flung her hairbrush across the living-room, aiming at Ross's head. It missed, but Ross yelled as if it had split his face open. He lunged at Rene and knocked her off balance. Rene kneed him in the chest and clawed at his shiny blond hair, the hair she wished she'd been born with instead of her own dark mop which never did anything she wanted it to. Alma, her mum, thundered down the hall and flung open the door.

'Right, that's it! Get your coats. We're going out. And no buts.'

'It's the holidays!'

'Too bad. We're going out.'

'No we're not!'

'I'm not asking you, I'm telling you.'

Rene and Ross immediately began to accuse each other of everything they could think of: starting the fight, sitting in the seat the other had first, using each other's stuff without asking, annoying each other's friends, ruining each other's lives. As always, the list ended up with Ross wishing Rene dead and Rene wishing Ross had never been born. Then both of them turned on Alma.

'It's all your fault!' they screeched.

Rene saw her mum draw in her breath sharply and bite her lip.

'Let go of your brother's hair, Rene.'

'He's not my brother!' Rene snapped. 'I don't have a brother. I've only got a half-brother and he's only half human.'

'Why do we have to go out? You're always trying to get us to go out,' Ross whined, in that maddening, brattish voice he resorted to when he didn't get his own way. He was nearly twelve, only two years younger than she was, but he'd need his birth certificate to prove he wasn't an overgrown five-year-old.

'And it's raining,' he continued. 'Pouring! Bucketing! Chucking it down! It's a monsoon!'

'We don't get monsoons here, stupid,' said Rene.

'Wish we did. And you got drowned in one.'

Rene flopped down on the couch. She didn't want to go out either. Not yet, anyway, not just after breakfast. She felt like lazing about, watching TV, reading her new magazine, phoning up some friends. If one of them wanted to do something she might have considered going out, but trailing off somewhere with her mum and the bratbrother – no way.

The programme she'd been trying to watch finished and the news came on. It was about the war. A reporter in a flak jacket was firing out facts about a bombed embassy and a village which had been set on fire. There was footage of a long line of refugees, heads bent, feet dragging, trudging over a snow-covered mountain pass, then it cut to a camp on the other side of the mountain.

Surrounded by high wire fences, the camp was a muddy wasteland already bursting with tired, sad, hungry people.

Alma picked up the remote and switched off the TV.

'Get your coats, please,' she said in that odd, small voice which Rene knew meant she wasn't going to change her mind.

They passed the hospital and the library, the gardens and the art gallery. The windscreen wipers clicked rapidly from side to side, like the metronome the music teacher put on to try to make Rene play in time. Rene hated that bullying, ticking box which made every tune sound like a march: left-right, left-right, eyes on the music, fingers on the keys, hup-two-three-four, hup-two-three-four.

As they crossed the main road, shoppers spilled off the pavements on to the street, nudged forward by the crowds behind them. Alma drove slowly across the junction, peering through the streaming windscreen. A man dressed in a hooded raincoat was holding up a big sign on a stick. The sign had a red arrow and the words

Golf Sale. He was always there, that man, on the exact
same spot on the pavement. Sometimes he tried to read
a book as well as holding up the sign but usually he just
held up the sign. What a boring way to make a living,
Rene thought, almost as bad as begging. A couple of
beggars were propped against shopfronts, huddled under
sodden blankets. They must have been freezing. Though
the clocks had changed and it was officially summertime,
there were white slivers of sleet in amongst the rain.

Nobody had said a word since they got in the car.
Ross had snorted and humphed and kicked at the car
seat. The *upholstery*, as her mum insisted on calling it.
Rene hated it when her mum used squirmy words.
There were plenty of normal ones which everybody
knew. Saying upholstery when you could say car seat
was just showing off, wasn't it? The word which really
made her toes curl was *step-sibling*. Everybody knew
what half-brother and half-sister meant. Step-sibling
sounded like some kind of dancing gerbil. And *alternative
lifestyle*, well that was a joke. As she'd had a dictionary
exercise on the last day of term, Rene knew the exact
meaning of alternative: *A possibility of choice, esp. between*

two things or courses of action. What choice had she ever been given, what alternative to her alternative lifestyle?

'I wish I lived with my dad,' she said loudly.

'I wish I lived with mine,' Ross piped up. 'Then I wouldn't have to see you every day.'

'Yes, you must do, sometimes,' said Alma, as she stopped the car at the next set of lights.

Rene growled. She didn't want her mum to be calm and reasonable. She wanted a fight. The windows had steamed up. Rene tried to draw a snarling face on the glass but somehow it came out more like a twisted grin. She wiped it away with the palm of her hand and looked out at the fancy city centre shopfronts. One had Japanese or Chinese writing on it. It was called White Stuff and sold skiing gear, so Rene reckoned the pictogram probably stood for snow. In primary school a friend had taught her a few Chinese characters: happiness and friendship, moon and mountain. At the time she'd wished she were Chinese so she could think in pictures.

Next to White Stuff was a place called Fat Face.

'Hey, Ross,' said Rene. 'They named a shop after you.'

Ross jabbed Rene in the ribs.

'Stop it, both of you,' Alma said. 'Please stop it!' Rene could hear the wobble in her mum's voice as she strained to make herself heard above their yells.

They swished down the hill away from the shops and crowds. Just a lot of wet, grey buildings now, but Auntie Mara lived somewhere nearby. Going to Auntie Mara's would be OK. Rene might get to see her big cousin, Mina, hang out in her room and hear about the clubs she and her pals went to at the weekend. Ross would leave her in peace at Auntie Mara's, happy to slob in front of the TV with a slab of home-made cake and some hot chocolate.

'Are we going to Auntie Mara's?' Rene asked.

'No,' Alma said. 'Not today.'

'So where are we going, then?' Ross demanded.

'Wait and see.'

Where they were going, they soon found out, was a decrepit old warehouse in the middle of a muddy yard. In the yard, bulging cardboard boxes were being transferred from a fork-lift to a van by a skinny man whose long, bare arms were blue with tattoos.

'Mind your back, son!' he shouted at Ross, who had stopped to watch him nudge the pallet into position, then tip the fork so that the box slid down into the van.

'We're here to help,' Alma said, hustling them towards the entrance. 'Not to get in the way.'

'I wasn't getting in the way,' Ross began. 'And I don't want to help . . .'

'Oh shut up!' Rene snapped.

Their thin bickering was lost in the noise of people working.

Inside, the first thing Rene saw was a mountain of black plastic bags. It started halfway into the warehouse and rose lumpily right up to the roof. One or two of the bags had burst open and stray shirts, jerseys and trousers lay sprawled and stranded on the slopes. People were adding new bags to the bottom. Others were filling trolleys. More was going on the mountain than coming off it.

The depot was noisy and busy and confusing. People were hurrying in all directions, pushing trolleys taller than themselves or staggering under the weight of bags and boxes. Near the entrance, a man was hefting boxes on to another fork-lift. Sweat ran down his red face and dripped off his chin. Alma asked him if there was somebody in charge.

'No really,' he grinned, and wiped his face with his sleeve. 'But speak to Betty, there. She'll put you right.'

Betty was a brisk, steely wee woman with a crackly voice and a worn, liney face. Rolls of sticky tape circled her arms like bracelets. Round her neck, a pair of scissors hung from a chain.

'I'll put yous on the clothes team,' she said, ushering them towards the back of the depot. 'It's no hard but use your brains, right? I mean, they're no needing disco gear. And open-toed stilettos are no exactly ideal for trekking across mountains. Right, somebody here'll show you the ropes. Good to see the bairns pitching in,' Betty called over her shoulder and rushed off to supervise something else.

Bairns! Rene and Ross were a head taller than Betty!

Tables had been pushed together into a sorting area in the middle. Black bags were stuffed under the tables. An organised woman, who wore an apron over a smart suit, explained that what they had to do was empty a bag on to the table, sort the contents and pack them neatly into the boxes. The boxes made a kind of wall round the section. What each box was for had been written on a flap: baby clothes, children's, ladies' coats, skirts, gents' trousers, shirts, and so on, about twenty different categories.

Rene and Ross made a space for themselves as far away from each other as possible. Ross got hold of a trolley-load of loose shoes and began, slowly, to sort them into pairs. Rene wedged herself between a woman wearing a headscarf – who worked faster than anybody else and didn't pay much attention to what was written on the boxes – and a broad, breathy woman who sighed a lot, especially when she was sorting baby clothes. At first, Rene also took her time. By now, her friends were probably just getting dressed and beginning to think of something to do together and here she was, stuck in a cold, smelly, dingy depot, sorting out jumble.

As well as having to squeeze past people to get at the bags and boxes, it wasn't always easy to decide which box something should go in. Gent's or lady's coat?

Child's or teenager's? Remembering Betty's parting words, Rene inspected the footwear carefully. Should open-toed sandals really go in? Flip-flops? Slippers? Rene shuddered at some of the underwear. Who'd want somebody else's grubby old bras? T-shirts presented another kind of problem. Plenty were in good condition but most had logos and slogans on them. Even if it was clean and hardly worn, was it really OK to send an advert for German beer, or an Australian cricket team? What about Bart Simpson baring his bum or a promo for Megadeth or Iron Maiden?

'You wouldn't want to add insult to injury,' the woman in the apron said, which Rene took to mean no. Anything dodgy went into the rag pile or the stuff set aside for the charity shop. The range of stuff which had been donated was amazing, from disgusting old rags you didn't even want to pick up, to brand new designer gear, with the labels still on.

Before one pile of bags was emptied and sorted, another trolley-load arrived. Over the stacks of packed boxes, Rene could see that the tip of the bag mountain still touched the roof. There must have been hundreds of bags, thousands maybe. It would take days, weeks to sort through all of them, and with more arriving all the time . . . Once a box was filled it had to be moved out of the way, taped up, labelled in English and the language of the country it was going to, a language full of Ks and Vs and Ps. Betty had swung by again and asked for somebody clever to take care of the labels. Rene wanted to volunteer but not to admit to being clever, even if Betty was joking. The woman in the apron said she'd do her best with the labels, so that was that. Still, there were plenty of other jobs to be done and after a bit Rene realised that, in a way, she was enjoying the work. She felt sad when she thought about what it was for, but helping was better than doing nothing. Ross, too, had given up trying to skive. On the sly, Rene had been checking on him and the truth was that she'd never seen Ross work so hard. And without a word of complaint!

Rene and Ross took over the job of shifting the heavy, packed boxes into the aisle. They still weren't speaking but with everybody saying what a grand job they were doing and how proud of them their mum must be, their silent feud began to feel small and stupid. A tiny blue sleepsuit fell on the filthy floor. Rene picked it up.

'You used to have a wee suit just like this when you were a baby,' she said, holding it up to Ross. 'You were quite a cute baby, really.'

Betty showed up again.

'Right, folks. We'll have to put that stuff on hold for now. I've a shipment coming in, courtesy of Her Majesty's laundry. Needs to be shifted in a hurry.'

An hour later, Rene and Ross were still folding blue-and-white-striped prison shirts and plain blue trousers, discarding the torn and the stained – Rene was sure every blotch was a bloodstain – and packing them up. Hundreds of jail suits had been donated, all clean and, as the woman in the apron said, hard-wearing. But Rene couldn't get the picture out of her mind of people in that awful camp opening the boxes and finding they'd been sent jail clothes, prisoners' clothes. To lose your home and your family and then put on prisoners' clothes, that couldn't be right, could it? Ross was standing next to her, sorting and folding.

'They're just shirts,' he said, reading her mind. 'Just think of them as shirts.'

'I can't,' she replied.

'No,' said Ross. 'Me neither.'

Alma suggested that they took a break but neither of them would stop working until Betty appeared and ordered the whole team to get down to the tea room for a cuppa before the men scoffed all the sandwiches.

They all squeezed on to a couple of battered old couches in the smoky wee room where you could help yourself to tea, coffee, cans of juice, cheese sandwiches, crisps and tangerines. They sat for ten minutes, the smell of tangerine peel freshening up the stale air. Nobody said much during the break and when the woman in the apron announced that a plane was going out that night, everybody got up immediately and went back to work.

It was late in the afternoon. The bag mountain was a different shape now. It leaned over a bit to one side. It had lumps and bumps in different places, different shoes and jerseys and coats were scattered across the slopes but it was still a mountain. And it was their job to shift it. Rene felt tired and grubby. Her hair was sticky with sweat and grit and dust but she didn't care.

'Hey, fatface,' said Rene.

'Hey, frizzhead,' Ross replied.

Together Rene and Ross loaded a trolley and began to push it back to the sorting tables. It was hard work nudging it through the narrow passageways between the packed boxes but it was nothing really, nothing at all if you thought about where all the stuff had to get to, beyond those other mountains.

Ghost Track

CHRIS DOLAN

Daura used to be the best. She was mega. She's a solo act now, though her backing band is more or less the old Hunter's Eye – Martin McAweaney on drums, Tommy McAuley keyboard, Siona Blair bass. No Robbie Armour, obviously – and it showed. Her new single's a bit downbeat, and not a patch on the numbers he and Daura used to do together.

She was on the telly the other night and we all watched her, the whole family, and no one slagged me. It's the one good thing about what happened. Everyone's off my back now about Daura. Nicola – my sister – doesn't make those big eyes any more, or talk in that daft voice of hers. 'Look at wee Peter. He's gone all gooey. Is it love, Petey?'

Dad doesn't wink at Mum and go, 'I'm keeping my eye on that boy.'

The football guys used to ask, 'D'you scream at the telly every time Daura comes on, Petey boy?'

The girls in my class went, 'No one's got a chance with Peter. He's all Daura's.'

Even Struan, my best mate supposedly, said I just had a dirty mind. He bought the new Hunter's Eye album, too, but still thought I was too much into Daura. 'It's just her flimsy gear and the way she dances you like.' Not true. Fact was that Daura was absolutely the hottest singer, the best songwriter, most ultrasonic performer.

Anyone who knows about these things agrees that Daura had a perfect sense of timing. No kidding. I'm the proof. The week she chose to strike had already been a total bummer. Nicks was sneering and rolling her eyes at everything I did or said, being even moodier and more tragic than usual. All over some lanky dork in the sixth year who'd just given her the bum's rush. (Quite rightly, in my opinion. Though I'm not supposed to know about her stupid love life. I'm not supposed to know anything about anything. I hate that, don't you? Everyone keeping you in the dark.)

When the Queen of Agony took to moping in the bathroom for an hour at a stretch the old dears lost patience. I, on the other hand, had visions of her getting her finger stuck down the plughole. She was forever scraping out rings of hair from the sink, claiming they were mine and that I was a stinking leper who was falling to disgusting pieces. Perhaps she'd wiggled her finger too far down and some sewer monster from the X-Files had got hold of her, was sucking her down into his lair, slurping her straight into his slimy belly.

The rest of that week kept up the same pathetic standard. I got dropped from the third year First Eleven. Then failed a class maths test. Struan – who doesn't like to be associated with losers – started bodyswerving me. Dad was too wrapped up in Nicola's amorous problems to be bothered with me. All I had to keep me going was Hunter's Eye and Daura. And then even *she* turned on me.

The new CD, *Downpour*, had just come out. Easily their best yet. (And, as it would turn out, also their last.) In case you've been living on the planet Zog for the past three years, I should give you the Hunter's Eye biog. Daura's real name is Amy Lamont and her band used to be called Shindig. They didn't record anything and I was too young to see them live but the word is that they were a red-hot concert band. Rip-roaring electric jigs, rocky Celtic anthems, that sort of thing. Kind of like Runrig meets the Corrs with extra punch and blast power. I reckon they'd have been pretty excellent.

Then she teamed up with Robbie Armour. An obscure Irish bagpiper, of all things. But he did this weird stuff with techno effects and drum programmes. Big in the dance scene. Not that I'll ever know first-hand about that. The way things are going I'll be a hundred and eighty before my old dears let me go to a club.

So anyway, this solo piper with his futuristic synths and backing tracks and samples teams up with Shindig, forming the new band, Hunter's Eye. It's like Lovehearts shaken up with Irn Bru. Skoosh. Potassium and water.

Lara Croft meets Duke Nukem. Splat. Hunter's Eye are a back-to-basics rock line-up with a really thrashy, heavy grungy . sound overlaid with the wailing, psycho pipes of Robbie Armour, not to mention Daura's phantasmagorical squealing.

Daura and Robbie, it soon turns out, are not only musical soulmates but a big, media-hyped item. I can't be bothered with all that, but the tabloids followed them all over the shop and they made a big splash when they announced they were going to get married. Still, it was Robbie who got Daura into mythology. Ancient Celtic warriors and all that. It's totally zany. They wrote all these songs about battles and curses and gods fighting with each other. If Mrs McCallum taught history like that she'd get top grades from the whole class. Kings of Denmark invading Ireland sometime yonks ago and winning the first leg but then getting turfed out in the finals by Fingal, King of Scotland. (There's even a top-notch computer game designed after their songs. I've got to Level Eight, and once I work out how to eliminate the gruesome Dargo there'll be no stopping me.)

I'd gone to bed early on the Thursday night, hacked off with the world and everybody in it, and lay back and listened to *Downpour*. The title track – the last one on the album – is the best. It's about Armour and Daura – the real ones. Amy and Robbie took their names from some kind of princess and a warrior. I know all about them now. Tracked down in the library the book they based their songs on. It's supposed to be ancient bits of poetry rediscovered 300 years ago, but according to the introduction it's all a big con. Really just some saddo making it all up. Never mind, it's still pretty cool.

> *Rise, winds of autumn, rise,*
> *Howl, storm, howl.*

Martin McAweaney rattling out the beat on his drums like gunfire, guitar feedback yowling, Robbie's pipes doing this kind of war cry. Megabrill. Then, instead of the song building up like every other band in the world does, Hunter's Eye lets it die away, getting softer, fuzzier, Robbie taking the vocal and half-whispering:

Daura, sweet as the breathing gale
Deep sleep in the tomb.

I think I must have drifted off to sleep myself when Daura's voice woke me up. There was something different about it. Something I'd never heard before. It sounded like she was talking directly to me. I was fuggy and confused, the way you are when you wake in the middle of the night. There was no music, just Daura talking. Her voice was low and kind of hushed, but it filled up my room.

The hunter is far removed.
He is in the field of graves,
Beyond comfort, beyond return.

It seemed that her voice was floating in through the window which was open slightly. I would've got up to close it, but I was too freaked. There's something horrible in Daura's voice. It's definitely her, but she's kind of croaking, seething. The sweat turns cold on my forehead . . .

> *He bleeds; her comrade dies.*
> *Not to the world, but to her.*

And then it starts to get really spooky, because it's getting obvious that she really *is* talking to me . . .

> *Do not believe that I cannot see you*
> *Lying there in the night.*
> *I am not a child of hunters for nothing –*
> *My glances are arrows. My breath the rush of a mighty*
> *army.*

I want to leap out of bed, run out of the room, into my parents' room, or Nicola's, or the kitchen, anywhere to get away from her! Away from this horrible ghost of Daura who's haunting me. But I'm frozen solid, half-propped up, eyes popping out of my head, heart thundering. And what she's saying gets scarier and more personal all the time.

> *You who failed your sister;*
> *Give your father shame.*
> *Who are not fit to stand alongside your comrades.*

She knows everything about me! About Dad and Nicky and school and the football team.

I don't know how I fell asleep that night. I think I just sort of cut out, like a safety valve shutting my head down. In the morning, it felt like a dream. Like I'd been hypnotised, had some kind of hex put on me. The last thing I remember was half-sitting up in bed, shaking. The next, waking up with her voice echoing around my head . . .

> *You have failed the daughter of Kirmor, Once-Warrior!*
> *She dies alone, and cold, without pity.*

And the way she says the word 'Pity', stretching the word out so sounds a little like 'Petey' or even 'Peter'.

Mum recognised there was something wrong when she came in in the morning. But I told her I was fine and got dressed, eyeing the wardrobes and chests in my room, half expecting a bloodless, mummified Daura to leap out.

I didn't say anything at breakfast – looked paler and glummer even than Nicola. I didn't say anything either at school all morning. The boys would have had a field day. 'Peter's finally flipped!' they'd say. 'Being spooked by *Haunter*'s Eye.' At lunch-time, though, Struan accosted me.

'What's eating you, O Silent One?'

I had to tell *someone*. If I didn't, I'd crack up, be carted off. Struan listened to the whole story, but he could hardly stand still for wanting to run off and tell the other guys about crazy Pete's hallucinations. Soon as I'd finished my tale he burst out laughing, and turned to yell to the guys.

'Don't, Struan.'

He could see the look in my eye, and settled for just laughing at me, calling me a wimpo and shaking his head.

'Never heard of ghost tracks, eejit? Where have you *been*, man? Everybody's doing them these days. There's a few at the end of every Robbie Williams album – ask your sister. Did you leave your CD player running?'

'I don't know. Yeah, must have.'

'It's an extra track that's not listed on the box. They're nearly always pure garbage.'

My football in the yard during the morning had been truly woeful. Now – although I felt like a pure dullard – I was relieved enough to play a semi-decent after-school game. Walking home afterwards, I wondered about ghost tracks. First I'd heard of them. And this one sounded so personal. No music or anything, just Daura saying all those weird things – and that 'without pity' sounding just like my own name.

Back home, I went straight to my room and put *Downpour* on. Selected the last track, forward-wound it to the end. The disc didn't stop spinning and the timer kept notching up more seconds, then minutes. Struan was right – there must be more recorded on the disc. I let the CD play on silently while I sorted out my kit and began my homework. Ages later, Daura's voice slithered into the room again . . .

> *The Hunter is far removed*
> *He is in the field of graves.*

A ghost track. Very badly recorded – background hiss, and the levels on her voice all over the place. Very unprofessional. What a weird thing to put on the end of your album. I listened to the whole album again, but knowing what was tucked away at the end ruined it for me.

Then after tea came Struan's catastrophic phone call.

'Hey you. I've just listened to *Downpour* right the way through, and there's absolutely *no* ghost track on it. You're a pure spoon, so you are. Stay out of my way next week, schizoid.'

And the phone went dead.

I have to admit, I panicked a bit. I began phoning round everyone who I knew had a copy of *Downpour*, asked them to check it out for an extra unlisted track. An hour later the calls started coming back in. Damian – a fifth year who I swapped albums with from time to time – said there was none on his. Martha – a friend of Nicola's who was also into Hunter's Eye – reported in negative, too. After the fourth knock-back, I went in to listen to my CD again. It was still there, Daura snarling quietly at me.

I am watching you, traitor soldier,
Prowling still in your lair.

I began to feel a different kind of fear. Not spooky or ghostly any more, but a cold sweat that I was being singled out. That someone not just disliked me but truly despised me. It was the worst feeling I'd ever had.

I caved in and told my family the whole story. They looked disbelieving, but when I played them the track, and then put on the copy that Martha had brought round and which was identical in every way to mine except for the ghost track, Mum and Dad and Nick all sat, lost for words, looking around at one another, stumped.

Give him his due, the next morning Dad got to work. He phoned the record company. He found out Daura's agent's address, phoned him. He phoned the shop where I'd bought the CD. And then he phoned just about everyone else in the world who he thought might be able to shine some light on the matter. Then, together, we wrote off letters to all the same people.

For a week I wandered around still thinking that Daura, for some strange reason, had it in for me. Mum and Nicks tried to get me to stop playing that spiteful track over and over, but I couldn't. I kept listening for some clue. Some joke. Some way of understanding what the whole thing was about.

Replies to our letters and calls began to come in. Nobody had a Scooby what had happened. The record company wrote to say they were sorry for any distress that was caused. If I sent them the offending CD they would look into the matter immediately. Hunter's Eye's agent finally phoned up, inviting me to bring my copy of *Downpour* into his office where he would replace it and present me with a fifty quid token to purchase CDs and games.

On Monday after school Dad and I went to the address in the city centre. Big new shiny building with a café at the bottom. This cool-looking dude with a ponytail and a suit came down to meet us. He took Dad aside, and they talked quietly for a moment. Then he turned to me.

'Pete. Would you give your dad and me *uno momento*?

Tell them in the caff that Marco says you're to have whatever you desire.'

So there I was, left in the dark again, and feeling so hacked off that I almost didn't recognise her. Daura, on her videos and record sleeves, always dresses like some eco-warrior gypsy. Ragged and tattered dresses, plaid and thongs hanging from her hair and her arms and waist, leather sandals wound up to her knees, flashes of paint on her face. It wasn't Daura walking into the café and looking round, but Amy Lamont. Small, hair shorter and more neatly brushed than Daura's, no leather belts or tartan. She looked like one of my mum's friends. When she spotted me and turned fully round, I realised it was her. That distant look, like she was lost in some fantasy world of her own – who could forget it after the brilliant video for the 'Last of the Heroes' single?

She didn't sit down or anything. Probably wasn't even in the café for more than a minute.

'You Peter?'

'Uh-huh.'

'Yeah, well, sorry and that. One of those things. Couldn't be helped.'

She looked right through me. Like as if she were still on the telly and couldn't see out from behind her screen. I had thought that if I was ever lucky enough to meet the great Daura I'd be starstruck. In fact, I felt nothing. Just kind of let down.

'Well, anyway. See you,' she mumbled, and trundled off.

And that was that. She left me sitting there, alone, none the wiser. More in the dark than ever, in fact. As if she'd never been in at all.

My dad collected me from the café, handed over my fistful of tokens and about another twenty freebie CDs and video games.

'You didn't mind me going off like that, did you? The great Daura demanded to see you alone.'

Then, all excited, he asked, 'Well? How was it? Meeting your heroine.'

I shrugged and mumbled. Dad looked surprised but, wisely, changed the subject. He handed me a typed document.

'Mr Smoothie wanted me to sign this on your behalf. I told him it was your decision.'

Which was a pretty neat move on my old man's part, I reckoned.

The big bust-up between Robbie Armour and Daura was all over the papers a fortnight later. Turns out he had another woman on the side. Nothing came to light about the CD she'd recorded specially for him, dumping him via a ghost track. No one found out that, due to a mix-up at the studio, a young fan – *ex*-fan – ended up with the one copy of the album she had made specially for Robbie Armour.

I never did sign Ponytail's document asking me to deny all knowledge of the faulty CD and swearing I had never made a copy of it. I threw it away (and the tape, which of course I *had* made) after seeing Daura with her new band on telly. I'm into a different outfit these days – scorching young Glasgow decibel-blasters Damian tipped me off about. Daura's latest fan – believe it or not – is Nicola The Down-hearted. She sits and mopes by the CD-player. Given that I used to do something pretty similar myself, I shouldn't really slag her, should I? (Even if they do deserve each other, pathetic freaks.)

Notes in the Margin

THERESA BRESLIN

One of the disadvantages of having Malky as a friend was that shopping trips were a major problem. As soon as we went into any of the big stores on Princes Street the security guards started following us around. He played up to it of course, acting furtively, picking things up and putting them back in the wrong place, loitering near the till, until the guys with the walkie-talkies got fed up and slung us both out on the street.

It was the same at school. Malky just pushed and pushed till he reached the limit, and then he was out on a suspension until a 'guarantee of good behaviour' was given by his parents, which usually meant his father threatening to thump him silly if it happened again. Which it did, but he didn't.

Malky was my friend, my best friend, my only friend, but I didn't understand him, truly I didn't. He *liked* school. He was clever, brainier than me in fact. Did half the work I did and scored better in exams.

'Why d'you do it?' I asked him. We'd cycled up Arthur's Seat. He was on another suspension and I'd skived off for the day. The sun was setting, and below us Edinburgh was beginning to put on her sparkly evening dress.

He passed me the roll-up and shrugged. 'Dunno. Life's too boring. There's got to be something more than *this*.' And he swept his arm over Edinburgh, Leith, the Lothians, and beyond.

'What?' I asked.

He didn't answer.

A real 'Nowhere Man' my parents called him, after some ancient Beatles song. They didn't like me hanging around with him at all. 'Got no ambitions,' my mum tutted. 'And he'll bring you down with him.'

They had a university place in mind for me. In their

minds, that is, not mine. They helped me fill out the application form, I got accepted, got the grades, got in.

Just before term started I cycled out to my granny's house in Fife. Going across the Forth Bridge and up the coast road, the manic cry of seagulls in my head, my eyes blitzed by the crazy Van Gogh yellow of the rapeseed fields.

She called it 'the' university. 'I knew you'd be the one in the family to do it,' she said.

She made some tea and got out the biscuit tin. She could still manage that, at least, but when you looked into her face you could see that she was losing it. Her eyes milky with cataracts, her mind clouding up with the drifting mists of Alzheimer's.

'Your grandad would have been that proud of you. You going to the university.'

I sighed. I hadn't decided I was going for sure. Malky was talking of travelling round the world. I wasn't the travelling type, but it had occurred to me to go with him. 'No big deal,' I said.

She sucked in her breath sharply. 'Oh, you're wrong there,' she said. 'That's a very big deal.' She turned to me, suddenly lucid. 'It's one of the things that Scotland prided itself on. You always felt that anybody could get to go to the university. If you were brainy enough and if you tried hard enough, you could do it.' She looked at the mantelpiece where she kept Grandad's photograph. 'He'd have been that proud of you,' she repeated.

He'd been a miner. A reserve occupation during the war, so no photograph in uniform. Just a smiling face with serious eyes, a young man in his Sunday suit.

'He was handsome,' I said.

'He was that.' She smiled and became vague again.

We drank our tea beside her fire, then I got up to go. She had to reach up to hug me. She lifted a parcel from the table at the front door.

'Your grandfather's books,' she said. 'He'd have wanted you to have them.'

Saying goodbye to Malky was more difficult. Now that the rehearsal of school was over, scared, yet desperate to start our lives properly. Both of us restless. Neither of us sure what we were about.

'Where will you go first?' I asked him.

'Australia probably. I've got an aunt who emigrated out there . . . I'll see what turns up.'

'Keep in touch.'

'Right,' he said. Then he walked away, flicking his dog-end into the gutter.

He sent postcards. I hardly replied to any mail. From him, from home. That first student year was so full of new experiences, language, literature, love. Granny's letters became more and more rambling, her writing indecipherable.

Then one night the phone rang. It was my mother.

'It's your granny,' she said.

She didn't have to tell me.

'She's dead,' I said, my throat thick with unexpected tears.

'No fuss, just as she would have wanted. Your Aunt Sarah went in to get her breakfast in the morning as usual, found her in bed, passed away in her sleep.' A pause. 'The funeral's on Saturday. You'll come, won't you?' My mother's voice on the phone half pleading, half demanding.

'Uh.'

'She was very fond of you, you know.'

'I know. I know.'

'You were her favourite. She gave you my dad's books.'

Grandad's books. I'd forgotten about them. When I went home for the funeral I found them stuffed under my bed at home, still wrapped up in brown paper. I undid the string and opened up the parcel.

Biographies of Bruce and Wallace. Poetry, MacDiarmid, Burns. Pamphlets, Maxton and MacLean, the Red Clydesiders. Some were new, some second-hand. Poetry and music books bound in burgundy and dark green leather, gleaming with gold leaf, marbled end papers foxed with age. The prices were marked on the inside, two shillings . . . three . . . ten . . . twenty. One edition with corded bindings, thirty shillings. Old money . . . how much was that worth now? I reached over into my rucksack and found one of my student texts on social history. He'd been a miner at that time. What had he gone without to buy these? Food?

There was no way of measuring their worth now. The frame of reference had changed. The world, our nation, had moved on. I couldn't equate. According to my lecturer in social sciences I belong to the generation who don't reclaim the pound coin deposit from supermarket trolleys. 'What does that tell you?' he'd demanded. 'A week's wages for a working man in 1920.'

'Look who's here.' My mother was at my bedroom door, her voice determinedly pleasant. 'Happens to be home for a bit. Dropped by to see you.'

I glanced up. Malky. Tanned, thinner, hair in a ponytail.

He sat down beside me on the floor. 'Shame about your granny,' he said.

'Yeah.'

'What's all this stuff?' he asked.

'My grandad's books. She gave them to me.'

He sat down on the floor beside me and picked one up.

'She kept saying that he'd have been proud of me, going to university. Said he would have wanted me to have them. I never even opened the parcel till now. Some of them cost what must have been a huge amount of money then. He obviously loved books. I wish I'd known him, now I never will.'

'There's stuff written here,' said Malky. He held a book out to me.

I looked at the open page. There they were, written in careful script. Pencilled lightly, as if frightened to spoil the precious book, his notes in the margin.

The writing blurred. 'He never got to go to university,' I said.

'But you're there,' said Malky.

Now sometimes in a lecture theatre my mind drifts, and I wonder how Malky's doing. He's travelling again, somewhere in India at the moment. And here am I, at the university, with grandad's books.

Time Table

CANDIA MCWILLIAM

The story of what's happened at our kitchen table is the story of our family, as far back as I can remember it. That's good and bad things.

It's a square table, and it came from a sale in the Lanes, when my parents were young and starting off their lives in the house they were warned not to move into, because it was so wet there were frogs in the basement.

So they got a duck to eat the frogs, and another duck to keep the first one company, and then I came along to chum them.

They – my parents, not the ducks – called me Hugh and I thought everyone meant me when they said 'You' until I realised people were waiting for me to make the mistake and I got embarrassed. Later, when I wanted attention, I would try the old trick that had diverted them, but they wanted more by now, my audience, the grown-ups.

I'm a small man and I was a small boy. In the street were two gangs; one dedicated to those early investigations into human biology that scare children as they fascinate them, and one dedicated to minor vandalism and the persistent low-grade persecution of the very young and the very old – doorbell pushing and running away, abstraction of toys, those kind of things.

I exploited my only-child singularity by moving between these gangs, brokering information and lying through my teeth. I moved gang seasonally.

It was more fun in winter to be indoors, playing mothers and fathers and hospitals, and more fun in what passed for summer to be out and about, swapping milk bottles on doorsteps and totting ice lollies off weans in their perambulators.

There were perambulators back then, high things you strapped a baby or toddler into, that wallowed down the street and were too wide to pass one another on the pavement, so you'd to manhandle them down off the kerb and back, fighting the springy weight of metal and wadding and leather like someone hauling on a sail in a fat wind.

We spent most of the time hunting down cats to annoy and old pop bottles to redeem for tuppence – that's two d, which to you would be a fleck of dust on your trainers – so's you could spend the gains on the main thing in life – which was sweets.

Is it still sweets for all of yous, I wonder?

We loved frother bars, cherry lips, soor plums, puff candy, rhubarb and custard rock, sherbet satellites, McCowan's milk and toffee chews, peanut brittle, nougat that was like the soles of angels' sandals, cough candy, Highland toffee, lickrish ropes and watches and shoelaces and wheels and pipes, coconut baccy, sugar cigarettes . . . they were training us up for the next vices we'd take up after sugar, though the sugar never lets you go either.

So now I've given up sweets and I've given up cigarettes, but I've still that kitchen table I began on telling yous about.

Will you have a drink? I've sugar-free or the full Bru

from that machine over there, and there's some of that coffee that parches you up and is meant to have none of the bad aspects of the real thing. They'll be saying it aids a wholesome night's rest next thing, like that notice on the sweetie shop door: CRAVEN A IS GOOD FOR YOUR THROAT.

We believed what we was telt then, so now you see me, a wee man who believed in taking stout for his soul – MY GOODNESS, MY GUINNESS – confectionery for his metabolism – A MARS A DAY HELPS YOU WORK, REST AND PLAY – fags for his social life – YOU'RE NEVER ALONE WITH A STRAND.

We go on nowadays as though that was some kind of happy time when we were poor in a way that made us somehow rich at heart. But I don't know that everyone doesn't feel that about the time when they were young. I wish sometimes my other, nearer time had never happened to me.

Anyhow, how did I get started there? What did they want me in here to talk about to yous?

Oh, *you're* here to see *me*. My pleasure. Though they aye say it's Her Majesty's.

An object of importance in the history of Scotland, that's the one. That's what the museum man said, I mind, right enough.

If you listen, you'll maybe find out why.

It was not just any kitchen table.

I was raised at it.

You can laugh.

At that table, I cut out the pictures for my scrapbook with my mother, from her picture papers.

The word magazine didn't land till later. From America.

France if you say so, I'd not know. Sounds like guns to me. And *that* hard and pointed right at you, they were, that full of wee hooks and fixings and bolts and straps. The bras the women wore in they magazines; I mean, I cut them out.

Oh, I'm sorry, miss, I thought kids nowadays . . .

What's that about example? Why've you come to see me here if it's an example you're wanting?

To the table. I learned to count on it. On it I learned my habits of precision.

I watched my parents over that table, the slow way

they gradually stopped talking much, then spoke a lot and then one of them was aye there without the other, and then it was just her but the effect on the cooking was not, as I'd been hoping, to improve it for she was, more often than not, not in a fit state.

Oh, sorry.

But we agreed, did we not, that I'd tell you how it was in the Scotland of my youth? Or my bit of it. The bit where my ain folk sat. The table.

Oh we did not, did we not?

Well, here I'm and I'll say my piece now I'm here. It's only right.

No, I knew that few girls, but I'd aye been interested in the differences. Naturally, after my apprenticeship in the research gang down our street.

At the table we did other things than cutting out. I did mental sums my mother threw at me like someone at a hoopla stall. I mostly caught them and gave as good as I got.

No, never reading. I can't see it with reading. It's too free.

See, in my head, I don't want any ideas riding about

like riderless horses. There's a danger to it I don't care for.

Never saw the point to it. Pictures and figures, they're what you need, aren't they?

See a picture of a thing, find its price, want it, get it, hold it.

Best meal at the table was the first time I came out of being away. She'd excelled herself, down to the cabbage. For the dessert, there was shaky jelly.

That still breaks my heart.

She was a daft woman, my mother, in many ways but she stood by me and she made me shaky jelly, creamy pink with Carnation and raspberry jelly, all breasting out the bowl. And she let me eat it how I wanted, with my knife and fork, reducing it down slice by sweet wobbling slice.

No wafers, no ice cream, no fruit, no extra Carnation, just the bare pudding in its deep cupped bowl.

The relevance of the table is coming. Have you not heard of suspense?

Later, when she was not what you'd call resigned, but she was still that attached to me she couldn't take her eyes off me once, she asked me outright what it was that inspired me to my hobby.

I said, 'You, Mother,' and she looked scared.

'Maybe if I'd've had a sister, I'd've been able to help myself,' I said and she closed her mouth firm for by that time she was on the twelve steps programme for the booze and kent fine that it was my responsibility and mine alone if I insisted on leading the life I did, with all the demands it made on me – routines and checks and research. And night work.

She didn't like it that I often had to be out alone and at odd hours by now and she took to worry as she had to drink.

For some reason, she began to make connections.

I would find her reading newspapers, even marking them.

When I come in – yes, came in – she'd scrumple the papers up hard as though that was her main purpose, to reduce her reading matter to stuff for polishing windows, all those dirty words used to take the smears off the windows' glass and bring them up clean as no glass at all, just lovely transparent air.

She'd become jumpy, too, asking me if there was anything I'd like to say.

Well, no, she was my mother, wasn't she?

Do yous tell your mothers everything?

Well, maybe your heroes would, maybe they would not. I don't see Graeme Souness and Prince Charlie and the man off of *Trainspotting* legging it over to tell their mother each and every time they get an urge.

Leave alone someone in my line of country.

Where I am now, the room just down the way in my part of this place, they let me have the table.

Just the one thing.

It's a benefit of life.

Not of every life, no.

But of being in for it, see.

This table of which I speak, young ladies, young gents, was the childhood table of a man whose *métier* – and *that*'s French, right enough – was an unusual one.

Very well, gentlemen, I shall not go into detail, but what is the use of my very special qualifications if I do not use them, as very few can, to pass on the lesson I learned from my years in the processed tragedy business, as I call it, which is that anyone at all, even a wee man with but a table to his name and no vices but the one, can yet end up with a career in education.

I'll be off with my friends now. And here now, look at me. Do I no look normal till you see the cuffs?

So that's your lesson.

What do you say?

That's as may be.

I've always been perfectly normal except when roused to anger.

In case anyone's asking, I don't take tea or coffee myself. I make it my business to steer well clear of stimulants.

The Five Sisters of Kintail

JACKIE KAY

The reason I am writing this story at all is because I am in hospital and I'm bored out of my tiny mind. The reason I am in hospital is because of the story I am about to tell. The reason my mind is tiny is because it has been eaten by my pals.

Let me tell it like it is: the truth, nothing but. I am no good at making things up. My imagination just died on me the day it all started. The day that led me to be lying in this bed here with the white sheet over my body; a tight needle carrying antibiotics into my veins; a strange table on wheels for eating the sad dinners that you choose from the menu card the day before. A hand-controlled gadget with a red button to press for calling *Nurse* and a black button to turn off my light. If the black button could turn off my brain, terminate my memories, grab the terrible whirling inside my head, I'd be happier in the night. It's never quite dark in hospital. Lights come from the nurses' station; patients appear to glow in the dark.

There are several sockets above my bed reminiscent of 'ER' or 'Casualty'. If my condition worsens, there are enough sockets there to plug in the ammunition they'd need to keep me going. There's a small oxygen cylinder resting in the corner with one eye open. There's a bowl of fruit with two bananas going brown, one red apple, one orange. There's a jug of hospital water with a blue lid. Even the water tastes sick. I don't sip it. I don't touch my fruit. I stare at my four cards from time to time. They are from the four others. They intrigue me. Is it not a bit late for pity?

I am freezing cold even though they tell me I am raging hot. They won't fetch a blanket. I swear the sheets are stained with somebody else's blood. I'm burning up. The nurses say, 'Dear oh dear, you are burning up.'

Today, I was thirty-eight point seven. 'Not quite out of the woods,' the nurses say.

I say, 'I thought you said I was in a hospital.' And they laugh.

'I can see we've got a smart Alec here.'

I am hallucinating my own name. Through the open hospital window, I hear it being called. *Saucy Mary*. I look out at the trees in the sunshine. A man attached to a stand-up drip thing on wheels is actually sitting on a bench smoking. Bampot. But no sign of them. The ones who gave me my name.

For so long they were my best friends and everything was fine. I can't really start with meeting them. What mince! I can start where I like. It's my story and I'll cry if I want to, cry if I want to . . .

A nurse just popped her head in there to ask me if I was all right. Apparently I was singing my sick head off.

There were five of us. We called ourselves *The Five Sisters of Kintail* after those dramatic looking mountains hanging gloomily around Kyle of Lochalsh overlooking Loch

Duich in the Highlands of Scotland. We climbed those mountains on our school holiday. We were a gang. Items. A girl gang. Other girls in twos and threes envied us. Solid. *Don't mess with us*. We were tough. We weren't joking. There were some girls that would shake a bit when they saw us. But we just laughed in their faces and said things like, *Get a Life, Wee Girl* or *You Got a Problem? Or What's She Staring At?* But we were harmless really. Big soft girls really. Each of us still slept with a teddy. We've all got the same one that we bought in Skye, that same holiday. Tartan scarf round the neck.

Let me introduce us, then. Me, Saucy Mary. Sheila na Gig, Mabs, Lizzie, and the other Mary, our Queen, Mary Scott. It happened like this: Sheila got hers first and kept quiet about it because she was only ten at the time. Her mother hadn't told her yet and so when she woke up she was convinced she was dying. When Lizzie got hers next at twelve, Sheila said, ever so casually, 'Oh, I've had mine for a while.'

The sisters rounded on her. 'Since when? Liar! Pants on fire!'

'I don't use pads,' Sheila said convincingly. 'Pads are

for babies. I use these,' and she pulled a cotton wool bullet out of her bag. 'Lil-lets,' she said.

'How can they hold the blood?' I asked, appalled. 'Too wee.'

'Come here and see this,' said Sheila, enjoying her moment of glory.

We traipsed after her to the bathroom where she ran the bullet under the tap and the whole thing swelled with water. 'It swells inside you,' Sheila said triumphantly.

'Why didn't you say before?' we all asked Sheila.

'I was too embarrassed. I was only ten! I thought I was too advanced for my age.'

The Queen looked like she could burst into tears. Sheila was so 'advanced' she avoided the padded bra. 'I don't need mine any bigger. Look at me!' she'd say.

Mabs' period arrived when she was thirteen and a half. I could tell the Queen was really upset about it all because she kept talking about it. *Obsessively*. Asking me if I'd had any 'spotting' or strange stomach cramps or diarrhoea. All signs of the blood's imminence, apparently. I wasn't too bothered until the Queen started on. She said she should have been first, being the Queen. She was right worked up about it all. Until she got her first period, it was like a competition between us. I was relieved when the Queen's period arrived before mine because I knew the spite and the jealousy would have been unbearable. The Queen was fourteen and two months.

And so the blood came for all the blood sisters but me. I was long and skinny and had no hope of filling a bra for a long time with anything except padding. My body was all bone and muscle, no flesh and blood. I was different in every way from all of my friends. But, I consoled myself, at least I had friends.

I might have been all right, but my own gang started to pick on me. A bit much, really. One of the reasons for hanging out in your own particular gang is to protect you from that sort of thing. But the Kintails didn't see it like that. At first, it might be called innocent teasing. But then it developed, grew, expanded, exploded, and before I could say *blood sister* my life was hell.

The Queen would sidle up to me in school and whisper, 'Mary, I'm worried about you. Have you not got your period yet? Oh dear! You're the last in the whole school! Even girls in the year below and the year below that have got theirs.'

Then Lizzie would saunter up and say, 'Seriously, Mary, we're all really anxious about you. We're losing sleep. Better get your mum to take you to the doctor. Better see the doctor.' And Lizzie would shake her head and tut and then Sheila would start.

'It's really bad. If you don't get them soon, you'll never be able to have children. You have to get them before you're fifteen.'

'What's the big hurry? I'll have them for the rest of my life,' I'd say.

The thing about teasing is the way it starts is not the way it finishes. I don't know that the Kintails ever did decide for things to go so far. I'd like to think not. I think the others were egged along by our bad Queen. Mary Scott liked it if one of us was in the huff with the other – 'no speaks'. I'm not sure what was up with her. Maybe it was a gene thing. Her mother was the most snide woman in our neighbourhood. Mary's mother noticed the wrong things about people all the time. With pleasure. 'Is that all she got for her birthday? Parents must be feeling pinched. Mind you, they spend enough on themselves,' Mary's mother would say.

Whenever Mary's mother got something new, she'd walk round the block to show it off. 'There's Irene showing off her new cashmere coat,' my mother would say grimly.

One night we were all coming back from the youth club, walking down Maryhill Road in the twilight, when Mabs said to me, 'Is your sight all right, Saucy Mary?'

'Yes . . . why?' I said.

'Oh, nothing. I was just reading that the sight starts to go if you haven't had your period by fifteen.'

The Queen joined in, delighted that Mabs had initiated round eleven. 'You become blind and infertile, barren, no man wants you. Oh, Saucy Mary, pray they come soon.'

I did all sorts of things to check my sight. When I was waiting for a bus I was sure it took me longer than before to recognise the number. I tried reading the writing on billboards from a long way off. I slept with the bedside light on at night because the dark scared me. I never looked up at the sky because it seemed too bright.

One Saturday morning I was packing my swimming cozzie in my bag ready to go for our usual swim when the Queen turned up at my door alone. 'Sorry, Mary,' she said. 'We can't risk swimming with you any more until your first period arrives. See if it arrives in the baths, we'd all end up swimming around in a flood of blood. It's taken so long to come, it's bound to fill the whole pool. Three years' worth in one go. It's not for the Kintails, Mary.'

I knew she was talking rubbish, but I didn't want to give her the satisfaction of arguing with her. I didn't say anything. I was silent. I could feel my lips go thin with disappointment. 'Suit yourself,' I said, and closed the door on the Queen's face.

I went up to my bedroom, punched my pillow and cried.

'Not going for your swim?' my mum asked me later that afternoon.

'I don't feel like it,' I lied.

'Is there anything the matter? I know you,' my mum said sympathetically.

'Nothing,' I hesitated. Then I said, 'Nothing,' again.

The Queen sent me a note the first period of the day. *Periods arrived yet?* It never occurred to me to lie. 'No,' I shrugged.

Mabs grabbed me in the toilets in between double maths and double history and said, 'Mary, maybe you're a hermaphrodite.'

Lizzie said, 'Are you going to turn into a man?'

Lizzie was my favourite. The others left and Lizzie lingered. She looked sorry that she had just said what she said. She blushed. I grabbed the opportunity. 'Don't do this to me, Lizzie,' I said. 'You're nice. You've never got anything out of place. Your hair is always just so. Your eyes are nice.' Lizzie was astonished. 'What's a hermaphrodite, Lizzie?' I asked.

'I don't know but it sounded pretty bad,' Lizzie said.

We laughed and Lizzie hugged me impulsively. 'I'm sorry, Mary,' she said. The Queen walked in. Her eyes were all flash and glare. Something really nasty shone in them – something that told me my life would be worse than worthless from then on.

Lizzie left us to it, rushing towards classical studies. Mary had always hated anybody in the Kintails being closer to another than to her. She liked control. She went bananas. She grabbed hold of my hair and yanked me about the toilets. She called me names. 'You are going to be expelled from the Kintails!' she threatened and rushed off to home economics.

I went to Mary's house that Friday night. I was told to be there by seven or she would tell the whole school I was a '*lessie*'. All the Kintails were there. Mary's parents were out. We sat around her floor in a circle. Mary turned off the lights and lit a candle.

'I hereby expel Saucy Mary from the Kintails,' she said.

All the others had to say, *Away you go, Saucy Mary*.

The Queen took a pair of scissors and cut a big bit from my hair. 'This is the hair of an ex-member. It will go in the jar of ex-members' hair.'

She handed the lock to Lizzie, who opened up the jamjar and put my lock inside without looking at me. 'Rise, Mary, rise,' said the Queen. We all stood up. The Queen opened the door and shoved me out. I wept all the way home in the dark.

The rain was bouncing off the ground. I could feel it go right through me. My back was soaking wet. The rain was falling down my face. I kept stopping to wipe it and then run on. I could feel the freezing cold right through to my bones. It all felt like punishment. I stopped for a moment and stood with my hands held wide out in the black night rain. 'Soak me,' I said. 'Soak me right through.'

When I got home, I tried to sneak up the stairs unnoticed but my mum pounced on me. 'Mary! You're soaking! You're absolutely drenched.' I started shaking and shivering. I was shaking uncontrollably. I didn't say anything about the Kintails. It was one of our rules. Never get one of the gang into trouble. Never grass, never leak, never spill, never tell, never sneak, never betray. I couldn't speak. The blood sisters had sucked me dry.

I think it was that night or the night after that, that my mum called the emergency night doctor and the doctor called the ambulance and I drove in the dark, staring out of the black windows of the ambulance. I thought to myself, *Take me away. Take me away.*

Yesterday Lizzie came to visit me. A bunch of yellow flowers in her hand. She sat at my bedside looking very dramatic, very serious. I think she thought she was in a movie. She held my hand like I was dying or something. 'The doctor told your mum it was very grave,' Lizzie whispered. 'Oh, Mary, I'm sorry. Sorry, Mary, I'm sorry.'

'Are you sorry?' I said, managing an ironic smile.

'Mary's father's left her mother for a much younger woman,' Lizzie announced dramatically.

'Really?' I said.

'Yes, a blonde secretary,' Lizzie said, relishing the older words. 'A *bimbo*, her mum said,' she added, daringly.

'Oh,' I said.

'Look, Mary, things just got out of hand,' Lizzie said, trying again.

I smiled weakly. My mum came in and took the flowers. 'Freesias,' said my mum, sniffing. 'How lovely. What good friends you girls are.'

Tonight I went to the hospital bathroom for the first time. Scary place. Silver rails to pull yourself up if you're not able. Before that I'd used this cardboard potty that the nurses brought to my bed. Most undignified and unladylike. I hobbled down the hospital corridor. It was there, in that hospital bathroom, that I saw it for the first time. *Hallelujah*. The menstrual blood! I had a strange wobbly feeling. I started singing, 'Glory, Glory Hallelujah' even though I'm not religious.

The nice nurse had heard me singing. 'You sound cheery tonight.'

'I've just got my period.'

'Right,' she said, looking at me oddly. 'And are you always this delighted when you get your period?'

'This is my first,' I said, shyly, proudly.

'Oh well then,' the nice nurse Vicky said. 'Congratulations and celebrations!' she sang, sweeping about my curtains.

'Wait till I tell our Queen,' I said to the nurse.

'I know it's important to you, but do you think the Queen will be interested?'

'Definitely!' I said confidently.

Granny's Books

GORDON LEGGE

> One of the most important of women's duties is to make
> the most of the fruit which grows in the gardens and
> hedgerows. To do this efficiently we must be ready to
> preserve these fruits as they come into season. The most
> usual method of doing this is boiling with sugar, either
> in the form of jam or jelly.

Even when Mary was wee, the book was old. Its pages
bound by a length of knotted string, it would hang from
a nail in the kitchen cupboard. When the cupboard door
was opened, the pages would flap. Mary could never

remember the book having a spine or a cover, just that length of knotted string.

Time was when every home had just the one cookbook, the recipe book, the WRI recipe book. Following its simple instructions, Mum would bake for visitors: Empire Biscuits; Jack Frost's Snowballs; Coconut Shortcakes. Always treats. Then there were the puddings, puddings for the family: Lemon Meringue Pie; Baked Rhubarb and Tapioca; Steamed Apple Pudding.

But if there was one thing Mum was famous for, it was her jam, the raspberry jam. Every year Mum would make raspberry jam. Enough to feed an army.

Now, for the first time – and probably the last – Mary, too, was making jam, raspberry jam.

Like the book said you should, like Mum used to, Mary wiped 'the inside of the preserving pans with a sheet of well-buttered paper'. Mary had bought two pans especially for the job.

They always said Mum's jam had lots of seeds in it. This was supposed to mean you were a nice person, a kind person. It was like a superstition or something.

Raspberry had most seeds, the biggest seeds, seeds that got stuck in your teeth. According to the book, raspberry was easiest to thicken. When making strawberry, you could, as a thickener, add rhubarb or jelly. But, as one of the contributors pointed out, this was 'cheating'.

Mary rinsed her fingers. As she did so, footsteps started to bounce down the stairs. Footsteps that, even if they tried, couldn't be any louder. Like somebody falling, like somebody being pushed.

One of these days, thought Mary, just one of these days . . . But no, this wasn't the time for an argument, for yet another argument.

'What you doing?' Caroline's eyes saucered as she caught sight of the table and worktops. 'This place is a midden.'

On the table: the preserving pans, the raspberries, the bags of sugar and the empty cartons. On the worktop: the jars with their stickers, the scissors, the thin paper lids and the rubber bands.

Caroline repeated, 'What are you doing?'

'Jam. Making jam.'

'Jam? But you never make jam.' Caroline laughed.

'What we going to do with all this stuff? You volunteered to put up refugees or something?'

Mary indicated the book, the WRI recipe book. Without having to look at it, she quoted from its pages. *'Make preserves in times of plenty.'*

Caroline had a blank look.

Mary explained. 'OK, Safeway had a two-for-one. Maybe went over the score a bit. It'll keep, though. Can always give it away.'

Caroline picked the book up. She held it by the string, at arm's length, as though it was contaminated. 'Exciting, exciting,' she mocked. Then she added, 'I take it this was Granny's?'

Mary nodded. 'It's older than me, you know.'

Caroline made a face. 'Looks it.' She put the book back down on the worktop. Using only the tips of finger and thumb, she carefully flicked through some pages. 'What's Apple Amber Pudding?' she asked. 'Who's Miss Birnie, Meigle WRI? Where's Meigle? Mrs Hendry, Paxton WRI. Where's Paxton? And what's WRI anyway? Wait, here's a good one. Steamed Five-Cup Pudding. What's a Steamed Five-Cup Pudding when it's at home?'

Mary shrugged. 'Haven't a clue,' she said. 'You tell me.'

Caroline mumbled the ingredients, then, in an exaggerated Dracula voice, read aloud: '*Soak tap-i-oca in milk . . . add bread-crummmmbs . . . su-et . . . su-gar . . . mar-ma-lade . . . and so-da. Put . . . in-to a butt-ered ba-sin . . . and steammmmm for two and a half hoursssss.*' Caroline made a spooky noise. 'Hold on,' she said, '*two and a half hours*? For a pudding? Haven't these people heard of Sara Lee? Eh, thanks, but no thanks. Total minger, like.'

Caroline went over to the sink. She washed the tips of her finger and thumb.

Mary said, 'You off, then?'

'Tasha's.'

Tasha was Natasha. When Natasha phoned she would say, 'Can I speak to Liney, please.' Tasha and Liney, like graffiti waiting to happen.

No, thought Mary, don't start. Not an argument, not now. It's always too easy to take things out on those closest to you. Like the book said – never pick a quarrel, even when it's ripe.

Fingers done, Caroline started putting on some make-up. Mary always left some make-up on the kitchen windowsill. 'Uncle Paul said there were two books. What's the other one?'

'Oh . . .' Mary made a flustered gesture with her hands. She didn't know what to say. Didn't know if she should tell or not. Not yet, she decided. 'Just an old book. A book of your granny's.'

Make-up applied, Caroline moved on to her hair. This time, using her mother's brush. She finished by putting a clasp on. 'We having pizza? We got pizza?'

'Think so. When'll you be back?'

'Don't know. Later.' Caroline adjusted her skirt, the short skirt. Then she looked at her mum. 'You OK?' she asked. 'You seem a bit spaced.'

Mary responded too quickly. 'Fine. I'm fine. See and don't be late, will you?'

'What was it, anyway?'

'What? What was what?'

Caroline rolled her eyes. 'The other book. The book Uncle Paul was on about. He said there were two. What was it? Tell me.'

'Oh, nothing. Just an old book of your granny's. Look, tell you later, OK?'

Caroline snapped her chewing-gum. She looked at the recipe book. 'You going to be making more stuff out of this?'

Mary laughed. 'Shouldn't think so. Just a one-off. Thought it would maybe be nice to make some jam. Granny used to make jam. Used to make it all the time. They say it was the best. Lots of seeds in it.'

Caroline snapped her chewing-gum again. She looked round, at all the jamjars, all the paraphernalia. 'But there's only the two of us. We'll never get through all this. You've got about thirty jars there.'

'Thirty-two. Told you. I can give some of it away. Paul'll take some. Grandad. There's plenty we can give to. Charities. That's what you do. You make jam, you give it away. Everybody tells you how great it is. Boosts the ego.'

Mary laughed.

Caroline didn't. She snapped her gum and said, 'OK, then. Take your word for it. I'm off. And remember, pizza.' Then she added, 'By the way, you *are* spaced. You are totally spaced, like. *Bye*.'

This time, Caroline laughed. Mary could hear her laughing all the way down the driveway.

Paul, Mary's brother, had been round at Dad's. Never one to just sit at peace, Paul would always end up getting them to do something, something about the house or garden.

Anyway, this day they'd been clearing out the attic, when they'd come across these two books. Paul phoned and said to Caroline that her mum would maybe want them or, at least, maybe want to see them.

That night, Mary phoned back. Paul told her what the two books were: the WRI recipe book, and their mum's diary.

'What?' Mary was shocked.

'Yeah,' said Paul. 'Mum's diary. Mum kept a diary.'

'But – she couldn't have. Mum didn't do things like that.'

'Well, the evidence would tend to suggest that she did. Look, do you want it or not?'

'Wait a minute, what d'you mean by a diary? What, for a year? She kept a diary for a year?'

'No,' said Paul. 'Not for a year. It starts when you were born, it finishes when you went to uni. It's all about you, sis. You're famous.'

'Come on. You're joking.'

'You heard.'

'But, what d'you mean, "It's all about you"? You've looked at it. What's it say?'

'No, I've not looked . . . Well, I've glanced at it. I haven't read it. You'll see for yourself. Bit of a weird one, eh?'

Mary stopped for a second, trying to take it all in. She couldn't. 'Come on, what you playing at? Am I supposed to see this? What does Dad say?'

'Sorry. Neither of us know whether you were supposed to see this or not. Look, d'you not just want to come round and pick it up? You can decide what happens with it.'

And that's what Mary did.

Preparation done, the actual making of the jam required little involvement, just a bit of watching. Start slowly, then boil, boil quickly. Mary began to tidy up. Putting away the cartons, wiping the table. The kitchen *was* a midden.

Before long, the smell took over. So strong Mary

could taste it on her tongue. There was nothing like long-forgotten smells to bring back memories. Mary remembered the old kitchen, the Bankside Court kitchen. Not the happiest of times. Mum that was always cleaning, Mum that never seemed to want for anything else. All these attitudes, all these 'duties'. Mary and her mum were always arguing. Different times, of course. It wasn't Mum's fault, that was the way back then, the world she'd been brought up in. It took Mary years to work this out, that it wasn't personal. If anything, it was political.

And, just as Mary had argued with her mum, Caroline, in turn, argued with Mary.

Sometimes, on a bad day, it seemed like all they ever did was argue.

Mary worked as a teacher in the local primary school. To save the embarrassment of being at the same school as her mother, when Caroline was primary age she'd got bussed out to another school, what turned out to be a better school. Until recently – a particularly bad day – Caroline had never mentioned how much she'd resented this, about her mum being a teacher, about being bussed away to the other school. Just who, she wondered, was this supposed to've benefited?

Mary had taken the diary to bed. Between its stiff, leather covers, yet no thicker than a jotter, lay the diary: thirty or so sheets of paper. Like the recipe book, the pages were bound at the corner by a length of knotted string. From start – *Mary was born* – right through to the end – *Today, Mary left for university* – was just one long paragraph.

The script was regular but tiny and difficult to follow. The paper was like tracing paper or kitchen paper – knowing Mum, it probably *was* kitchen paper – but the pencil writing was so faint it didn't come through. Every few lines Mary would come across a word she just couldn't understand – something that would look like, say, 'sausages' but, in context, couldn't possibly be 'sausages'. Then there were the blank spaces where words and phrases had just faded away altogether.

There were few dates. Just pointers: *Mary started school today*. A brief mention of Paul being born. The holidays. The times they'd moved.

Reading its contents, Mary got quite upset. This wasn't a diary, this was monitoring. There were things in here, written down, for anyone to see, that simply weren't true. Then there were the things that were true.

And these were the bits that upset Mary the most.

Earlier than expected, Caroline returned.

Something had happened. Without a word, she stormed up to her room.

Mary could smell the cigarettes. That chewing-gum wasn't fooling anybody.

The jam was nearly ready. The whole process had been much quicker than Mary had expected. Not the day-long activity she remembered. Five minutes more, then Mary would spoon the contents into the jars and apply the paper lids.

In the meantime, she'd go up and see Caroline. Not to find out what had happened, just to see if she could help.

Mary chapped the door. 'Can I come in?'

No response.

Gingerly, Mary opened the door. Caroline was standing next to the window. Again, the smell of smoke.

'You OK?'

Caroline's eyes were puffy. 'They said it again,' she said. 'They said it again.'

'What? They said what?'

'Said I look like a boy.'

This was what the make-up was about, the attention to hair, the short skirts. The other week, down the park, somebody, by pure accident, had mistaken Caroline for a boy. Her friends had latched on to this. Ever since, they'd teased her. They'd kept on teasing her.

'Well,' said Caroline, after a full minute of silence, 'you not going to say anything? Not going to give me a row for being stupid, not going to give me one of your patronising lectures?'

Normally, Mary would say something. After all, she was a teacher, that's what teachers did. They said things, they explained things, they encouraged debate. But this time, she didn't. Instead, Mary went over to her daughter and held her. Really tight, really close.

All she said was one word. She said, 'No.' Then she said it again.

There wasn't a pizza in the house. Caroline, feeling a bit better by now, offered to phone for one. Sure, said her mother, get garlic bread, milk-shakes, the works. The ice-cream van was outside. Caroline asked if she could go and get a video. Sure, said her mother, get two.

Mary was spooning the last of the jam into its jars. It looked good. Mary tasted some from the end of a spoon. Surprisingly, it tasted good as well.

The jars all filled, it was time to put the lids on and secure them with the rubber bands.

There were thirty-two jars in all, so thirty-two lids. The greaseproof paper lids. The kitchen paper lids. Mary examined her handiwork. The faint pencil markings were barely visible. Anybody taking time to look would just think it was a pattern. Most wouldn't notice at all.

To make the lids, Mary had cut up the thirty-two pages of the diary. Thirty-two pages, so thirty-two lids, so thirty-two jars.

A jar or two might linger in the bottom of the cupboard for a few years but, effectively, the diary was gone. Waste not, want not, as Mary's mum would say.

Caroline came in with a couple of videos. A few minutes later, the pizza delivery boy arrived. Mary and Caroline settled down in front of the television.

'Forgot something.' Caroline was up out of her chair. She went through to the kitchen, and returned with a pot of jam.

Mary laughed. 'Raspberry jam on garlic bread?'

'Why not? Could be good. Could start a whole new trend.'

Caroline spread a healthy dollop of the jam on to her bread, then tasted it.

'Well,' said her mum, 'the verdict?'

Caroline nodded. 'Good, really good,' she said. 'Plenty of seeds in it. Yeah, plenty of seeds.'

Mary smiled. Then tried some herself.

The Story of Major Cartwright, by Murdo

Iain Crichton Smith

Major Terence Cartwright, wrote Murdo, was an interesting man. He came originally from Hampshire.

When he arrived in the small Highland village of *A* . . . his first act was to learn Gaelic. Most of the natives had long ago given up speaking Gaelic but Major Cartwright was determined to keep the old traditions alive. He dressed in the kilt, made crowdie, cut the peats, and had a little dog called Maggie. The dog looked like a dishcloth which you might see on a kitchen table.

At ceilidhs Major Cartwright would introduce the singers and the songs.

'*Tha mi toilichte a bhith an seo an nochd,*' he would say, speaking with great aplomb. He would insist on speaking Gaelic throughout the ceilidh, though the natives were not used to it.

'We should not let these Sassenachs run our affairs,' he would say, when he spoke English. He voted Scottish Nationalist at all times and would say, 'It is high time we had a government of our own.'

He loved cutting the peats. Everyone else hated doing them: all of them used electricity, gas or coal. But to Major Cartwright cutting peats was the bee's knees. He was never happier than when he was out on the moor among the larks and the midges.

'A fine figure of a man,' the natives would say at first.

The Major made oatcakes, which the natives despised. He would hold his little dog in his arms and speak to it in the Gaelic. It looked like the bottom of a mop.

'*Tha mi uamhasach toilichte,*' he would say. A few of the natives initially disliked him: then more and more as they saw what he was up to. 'Anyone would think we were living in the eighteenth century; he is bad for our image.'

He advertised lessons in Gaelic but no one went. He wanted to teach the natives the correct use of the dative and the genitive, but they would have none of it. He even began to write poetry in Gaelic, which he published in a national magazine.

'Many is the time,' he would write, 'that I would look over to Harris of the lazybeds. It was there that I was reared.'

The natives thought that they ought to get rid of him. They felt he was riding roughshod over them. His poodle was stolen and Sam Spaid was asked to investigate. Sam Spaid hated the major at first sight and would only speak to him in English. He found the poodle on a washing line: Anna Maciver, who was eighty years old and almost blind, had hung him there.

'You senile idiot,' said Sam Spaid under his breath. 'You incontinent oaf.' He was wearing a black suit (from Anderson and Sons) and a pair of black shoes (from the Co-op).

'Here is your . . . thing back,' he said to the Major.

(You imperialist hound.) The major made crooning Gaelic noises to the dog, based on a lullaby from Iona.

'What are the marks on my dear Maggie?' asked the Major.

'Pegs,' said Sam Spaid curtly.

Sam Spaid went off in a rage to his next case. He had been paid in oatcakes.

The Major began to make oatcakes and crowdie for sale, but no one would buy them. He felt that he was becoming more and more unpopular.

At night, on his own, he read *Dwelly's Dictionary*. He knew the Gaelic for the birds and the trees and flowers, shellfish, and so on. Most of the Gaelic speakers from the village had joined the Gaelic Department of the BBC.

The Major had never been so lonely in his life, not even on Salisbury Plain. His wife had stayed in Hampshire and wrote to him in English. He replied in Gaelic. It was with great difficulty that he had managed to take the poodle with him.

'I did not find anywhere more beautiful,' wrote the Major. 'The lochs, the sheilings, the streams.'

He picked up his bagpipes and began to play the

'Lament for the Children'. In the distance he would hear the music from the disco, and someone singing 'Walk Tall' in an American accent.

It was one of his great sorrows that he could not find the Gaelic for 'poodle'.

Night fell over *A* . . . The Major put away his pipes. What had he done wrong? Whenever an Englishman came to the village he would say to him, 'This is not for you. You have done enough harm. Do you know, for instance, the Gaelic for "rhododendron"?'

The Englishman took the hint. After a while no one stopped in the village, and the bed and breakfast trade failed.

There were murmerings of discontent, rising to open roars of hatred.

'I was born in Uist of the peewit and the rowan,' wrote the Major. The moon shone over *Dwelly's Dictionary*.

One day with his poodle he left. All that was found in his house were some oatcakes, some buttermilk and some crowdie.

He went back to his wife in Hampshire.

Often he would look back on his days in *A* . . . with stunned amazement. He changed his poodle's name from Maggie to Algernon.

'We have seen much together,' he would say to him. 'The time is not yet. The books at the airports are all the same.'

He gave up the bagpipes and gave his kilt to Oxfam.

He and his wife opened a restaurant in Hampshire. His oatcakes, buttermilk and herring became famous. The menus were in Gaelic with English translations.

In the evening of his days he would say, 'Fine it was for me that I dwelt once in Harris.' An Indian was chewing his oatcakes with the air of a gourmet and a South Korean was delicately sipping his buttermilk.

'Fine it was for me,' he said, 'that I tasted the salt herring in my youth.'

Clearing my Head

I don't remember much about the journey home, except
that I felt very quiet and calm. Everything had changed.
When we stopped at the café in Dalmally for a cheese
scone (an end-of-holiday tradition) I was smiling. I can't
explain why. I just knew that things would be different
from now on. Not perfect, just different, and I was glad
about that.

We'd gone to Mull on holiday. At first it was just me
and Mum. That's not unusual. Dad can't normally find
the time. He says he will, every year, but at the last
minute he'll cry off. He's a TV camera operator and he

goes where the filming is. He's always sorry – genuinely sorry – but if the truth be told, I'm not. And neither is Mum. We never actually say it but somehow it's just easier on our own.

Mum had rented a cottage, a newly built bungalow on its own, close to the shore. It wasn't quite perfect – there were two steps up to the front door – but other than those I could move round all the rooms without help. Mum always feels very strongly about that. Old houses aren't made for wheelchairs so although this bungalow wasn't the traditional picture-postcard cosy highland cottage, it was great for me. That meant that Mum relaxed, and I love it when she relaxes. She's an economics teacher and although she always tells people how much she loves teaching, she loves holidays too. She says holidays clear her head.

The views from the house, down the sea loch and out towards the smaller islands, were brilliant. I used to think views were boring, a complete waste of time. Mum has always been big into views, and this year I began to realise what she meant. I loved looking out of the big picture window in the evening, watching the colours separate and merge, then flatten as darkness fell. Darkness doesn't really have a colour. It's like a blanket.

The journey to Mull had been fine – until we reached Oban pier.

Question. *How does Mum drive the car on to the ferry and push me up the gangway both at the same time?*

Answer. *She can't.*

There's always a horrible few minutes as she searches for some fit-looking person who'll take me on board. The guy she chose was perfectly pleasant to her about it and certainly did the job, but he didn't speak to me. That's not unusual though, and while I was waiting for Mum to appear from the car deck I was engaged in a very funny conversation by a transport-mad four-year-old called Moray. He kept poking about to find my gears.

We spent the first day quietly, pottering around, getting our bearings. Mum was winding down, and so was I. We talked a bit about my subjects for next year, planned a few trips around the island, read, recalled details of previous holidays, and looked out of the window. Mum drank gallons of tea. We were still and it felt wonderful.

In the evening, just as we'd finished clearing the dishes, we heard tyres crunching on the driveway and a hefty braking sound. Before I could wheel to the window to find out what was going on, the front door burst open and there was Dad, all bright-eyed and bushy-tailed.

When I say I'm not sorry when he calls off, it isn't because I don't want to see him. I love it when he's around. He's such a ball of energy and fun, it really fires me up. The problem is that I know it'll end, and that there won't be any warning. He'll just run out of steam and run off. Apologising like mad over his shoulder.

That night nobody said anything about the extravagance of his hired car. Mum didn't mention that she'd only catered for two. Neither of us asked for details about his sudden appearance. We were all just so pleased to see each other. Suddenly everything was exciting. We were laughing and joking. Dad had brought a brilliant new jigsaw of the ceiling of the Sistine Chapel – we're jigsaw-mad – and an Edinburgh version of Monopoly. It's hard to explain why but when he arrived we just adjusted to thinking about that very moment, not even five minutes ahead. You just can't rely on him to stick around, so it's as well to make the most of it.

When I finally got to bed – way past the usual time – my mind was buzzing. I thought I wouldn't sleep, but I did, until just after three in the morning. I woke to hear Dad walk carefully down the hall, open and close the front door and knew that the next thing I'd hear would be the car driving off. I got up and wheeled myself towards the kitchen, looking for the usual note. Mum was already sitting there at the window, crying in her sad, silent way.

'Don't ask,' she said to me. 'I don't know where he's off to.'

I was suddenly furious. The back of my neck felt as if it might explode, my hands were shaking and I felt rigid. I couldn't speak.

'And there's no point in getting angry,' said my mother flatly. 'It's the way he deals with things. It's not you.' She sounded so resigned. I'd heard her say something like that so many times but I didn't always feel like this. I wheeled myself back to my bedroom and slammed the door behind me before rolling into bed. I felt sore with anger and I couldn't fall asleep.

So I was awake when I heard the car return just after six.

We didn't talk about it. Dad simply said that he'd needed a breath of fresh air, as if it was the most natural thing in the world at that time in the morning. He was full of the joys, singing, shouting at the sheep through the window. I couldn't help laughing along with him, although I did feel strange, and sometimes a wave of that sore, cold feeling would wash over my head. But as the day wore on it happened less and less.

He stayed the rest of the week and it was brilliant. By the Thursday I wasn't even surprised to find him setting out the breakfast things in the morning, or to hear his dreadful whistling as he returned from a wet walk. We had the best holiday ever. The wettest too, probably, but you don't go to Mull for the weather in October. As we packed the car on the last morning I thought, This is my favourite place in all the world. I felt all moist-eyed as we drove away, and I knew it wasn't just the fabulous view that I was going to miss.

Dad pushed me on board the ship while Mum drove the car on. It was all so easy, so stress-free. We even went out on deck and sat with our fleeces zipped right up to the necks, our faces in the sun, watching the seagulls balancing on the wind. They fly at the same speed as the boat so they look as if they're floating.

And then this thing happened. And everything changed.

There was a daft woman floating around on deck, the kind of person you know is going to do something nutty and thoughtless. And sure enough, she did. She began throwing bits of her apple up into the air for the seagulls, but in a really stupid way so that they never managed to catch them. We were all exchanging 'what-a-wally' looks when she tripped slightly and dropped the apple. Mum and I got the giggles and she put an arm round me to give me a hug. Just at that moment, Daft Woman retrieved her apple and threw it into the air. It missed the seagull completely and fell between my mother and myself where it was squashed to smithereens by our hug. It was just a quick hug – the only kind I'll tolerate – but it was enough to mash the mushy apple into the sleeves of our fleeces.

The timing was perfect – if we'd been in one of Dad's sitcoms. We just laughed while Daft Woman was dancing around with bits of tissue. I turned to smile at Dad and I got the fright of my life.

He was standing with a truly scary look on his face, facing Daft Woman and her family and shouting at them, shouting, shouting, shouting. About apples, about idiots, about stupidity, about invisibility and about me. He went on and on and on and everybody turned to look at him in horror. Mum tried to calm him down but he pushed her away. I released my brake and wheeled over as best I could but Mum grabbed my handles and reversed me to the nearest turning point before pushing me to the other side of the ship. She hardly ever pushes me these days and I was furious at suddenly being in her control.

'Let me go. He should stop,' I said furiously over my shoulder. 'He's lost his marbles. That was an accident.'

But I stopped when I saw Mum's face. She put my brake on and fell to her knees beside me.

'This is the whole thing,' she said in such a tight voice it made me jump. She thumped the wheel of my chair with her fist with every word. 'This is his horror. Don't you see? This is what he can't cope with.' And she slipped over and sat on the deck with her back against the railings, eyes covered by her hands, her shoulders shuddering.

I was absolutely still. I felt as cold as ice, as if something strange had landed in my lap, something which might now explode. The shouting stopped and apart from the ship's engines the only sound was of seagulls. Dad appeared at my side, his face as stiff as a board.

'You OK son?' he said.

'No thanks to you,' I replied. He dropped next to Mum and I heard him say he was sorry. This time she pushed him away.

Five minutes passed and Duart Castle faded into the distance as the boat sailed on towards Oban. None of us moved. The rest of the passengers seemed to be over the commotion and Daft Woman was nowhere to be seen. Then Mum pushed herself up from the deck and sat on a chair, pulling me next to her. Dad came towards us and sat opposite, his chin in his hands, his elbows propped on his knees.

And then he began to speak.

'When I was at school, towards the end of secondary, a crowd of us went to a rugby match. Scotland versus Wales, I think. It was one of the good-natured ones. I remember one of our games teachers was playing and we kept shouting out, calling him 'sir'. We were having a great laugh. Then, out of the blue, this mutton pie came sailing through the air and landed slap-bang on my shoulder. The thing just shattered and then globbed, meaty, fatty, down my sleeve, down my front, and down my back. We all turned round to see who had thrown it. I could see the face immediately. Red, laughing from the depths of his belly, almost falling over with mirth at what had happened. My mates all began to throw abuse, but it was perfectly friendly. Not threatening. I was laughing it off. I wasn't even annoyed, although I knew my mum wouldn't be that impressed. We turned it into a big joke. I knew, walking home with the crowds from Murrayfield that day, that I'd remember that rugby match as the one where the mutton pie landed on my shoulder.'

There was a silence. Mum smiled with her mouth but not with her eyes.

'The thing was that I could, Matt. I could cope with that. I had pie on my shoulder but I wasn't left feeling an idiot. That stupid woman with the apple, she just didn't think. Didn't think about the effect on you. You *can't* move away. You can't say anything except, oh it's OK. People are so . . . *blind*.' He spat out that last word.

I suddenly understood what he was saying. I also knew that what he was saying was wrong.

'It wasn't on purpose, she was just larking around,' I said. I'd been going to leave it at that but something made me say more. 'You can't protect me from bits of flying apple any more than you can cure me and get me walking and running. Don't get angry with *her*. I'm all right. I'm almost always all right. Not perfect, not that mobile, but all right. So just get off my case.' I pushed him and he fell over on to his bottom. In other circumstances we might have laughed but we didn't. He just regained his balance and hunkered down in front of me again.

'I just can't bear it when that kind of thing happens,' he said.

I suddenly realised why he was always running away. I looked at Mum and saw that she'd always known. She was twisting her handkerchief round and round her fingers. The tannoy announced that the ship would dock soon. *Would vehicle owners please return to the car deck.* She got up and put her hand on Dad's head.

'See you two boys on the pierhead,' she said and headed slowly down the steps.

For a few moments neither of us spoke. My mind felt tangled and jumpy. I felt I really did understand what was going on, but that I couldn't organise my thoughts to get a grip on the facts.

'I'm OK, Dad,' I said finally. 'It's not easy but it's OK. And it's OK because of Mum,' I added fiercely.

'It's so hard to see you, Matt. Knowing this is as good as it'll ever be.'

'Not your problem,' I said harshly. 'I'm the one who's got to cope. If you don't like it, go away. That's what you usually do.'

There was a horrid silence and I felt strange and cruel. I knew that the next bit of the story was in my control. I was suddenly confident that he was going to stay and listen to me.

'If you'd stick around a bit you'd see that I manage. I go to school – and I'm doing OK there too, you know – and I come home and I have good mates and I have a life. It's just that you're not there. And you're telling me you can't be because you can't bear to see me like this. Well this,' I stabbed my index finger into my chest, 'this *is* as good as it gets. And it's not great but it's fine.'

His eyes opened wide and he grabbed my finger to stop me poking at myself, his head shaking from side to side. It was as if I'd given him the answer to something and in a way I suppose I had. He leaned forward, wobbling a bit, and put his arm round my neck and I felt all the coldness disappear. He wasn't perfect. I wasn't perfect. But we did belong together. It suddenly became perfectly clear.

So during that blustery, bright October day, my life changed. Everything changed. And that's why the three of us, slightly red-eyed and unusually quiet, could be found eating cheese scones in Dalmally, all of us smiling quietly and confidently.

Yes, holidays are great for clearing the head.

Biographical
Notes

Julie Bertagna was a teacher and journalist in Glasgow before publishing her first novel, *The Spark Gap*, in 1996. Since then she has written several books for younger children and another highly acclaimed novel for young adults, *Soundtrack*, which won the Scottish Arts Council Children's Book Award. Scottish Book Trust published her essay, *Towards a Creative Nation*, to mark the opening of the Scottish Parliament and the National Year of Reading in 1999.

Dilys Rose was born and brought up in Glasgow and now lives in Edinburgh. She has recently published her first novel, *Pest Maiden*, following several poetry and short story collections. She is a winner of the Macallan/Scotland on Sunday Short Story Competition and her first play, *Learning the Pasa Doble*, was premiered in Edinburgh's Traverse Theatre in 1999.

Chris Dolan writes plays, short stories and screenplays and has won a Scotsman Fringe First, the Macallan/Scotland on Sunday Short Story Competition and the Robert Louis Stevenson Memorial Award. He has been a writer in residence, mostly in Drumchapel in Glasgow, and published his first novel, *Ascension Day*, in 1999.

Theresa Breslin was born in Kirkintilloch and now lives in Lenzie, near Glasgow. She combines family life with her career as a writer and librarian. Her first novel, *Simon's Challenge*, won the Kathleen Fidler Award and she has gone on to win the prestigious Carnegie Medal for *Whispers in the Graveyard* and the Sheffield Book Award for *Death or Glory Boys*. Theresa is the subject of one of Mammoth's *Telling Tales* series of author biographies.

Candia McWilliam was born and brought up in Edinburgh. She now lives in Oxford. She is the author of *A Case of Knives*, *A Little Stranger* and *Debateable Land* which won the Guardian Fiction Prize. *Wait Till I Tell You*, published in 1999, is her first collection of short stories.

Jackie Kay's first collection of poetry, *The Adoption Papers*, reflects her own childhood in Glasgow – a black child adopted by a white Scottish family. A well-known and popular performer of her work, she has written several prize-winning poetry anthologies for young people and recently won the Guardian First Novel Prize for *Trumpet*.

Gordon Legge was born in Falkirk and grew up in Grangemouth in West Lothian. He currently lives in Edinburgh. He was the Writing Fellow at the Royal Edinburgh Hospital 1992–1994 and has published a number of novels and short stories. In 1992, *In Between Talking About the Football* was awarded a Scottish Arts Council Book Award and *The Shoe* was recently selected for the Scottish Library Association's Scottish Writers project for secondary schools.

Iain Crichton Smith was one of Scotland's foremost Twentieth Century writers, leaving a vast legacy of poetry, prose and drama in both English and Gaelic on his death in 1998. His readings of his stories about Murdo were always very popular, and he found them every bit as amusing as his audience, frequently succumbing to bouts of infectious laughter.

Lindsey Fraser grew up in Edinburgh. She worked as a children's bookseller in Edinburgh and Cambridge before returning to Scotland to work with Scottish Book Trust, the organisation which promotes the pleasure of reading and books to people of all ages. 'Clearing My Head' is her first published story.

Flame Angels

Edited by Polly Nolan

Freak? Flower child? True believer?

Who are you?

Coming home? Climbing mountains?

Where are you going?

Some of Ireland's best writers tell how the smallest thing can change your life, for ever.

Stories by Dermot Bolger, Herbie Brennan, June Considine, John McGahern, Marilyn McLaughlin, Joseph O'Connor, David O'Doherty, Michael Turbridy.

Family Tree

Edited by Miriam Hodgson

Is it a special bond, or a chain, that links members of a family? Is the best family the one which lets you be yourself?

A unique collection of stories about some very different families by ten of today's most popular, prize-winning authors.

Stories by Vivien Alcock, Tim Bowler, Melvin Burgess, Helen Dunmore, Anne Fine, Anthony Masters, Michael Morpurgo, Julie Myerson, Stephen Potts and Jacqueline Wilson.

Mixed
Feelings

Edited by **Miriam Hodgson**

Laughter, tears, misunderstandings, anger, frustration, discovery and loyalty are only some of the feelings these stories uncover in the power and complexity of the relationship between mother and daughter.

Stories by Vivien Alcock, Annie Dalton, Marjorie Darke, Berlie Doherty, Anne Fine, Jamila Gavin, Gwen Grant, Monica Hughes, Jean Ure and Jacqueline Wilson.

'*Mothers and daughters are like loving hedgehogs; full of warmth and prickles.*' Vivien Alcock